PUMPKIN EYE

For Marcia and Peter...

ISBN 0-439-38874-0

Copyright © 2001 by Denise Fleming. All rights reserved.
Published by Scholastic Inc., 557 Broadway, New York, NY 10012,
by arrangement with Henry Holt and Company, LLC.
SCHOLASTIC and associated logos are trademarks and/or registered
trademarks of Scholastic Inc.

12 11 10 9 8 7 6 5 4 3 2 1   2 3 4 5 6 7/0

Printed in the U.S.A.   09

First Scholastic printing, September 2002

The illustrations were created by pouring colored cotton fiber through hand-cut stencils.

Book design by Denise Fleming and David Powers

PUMPKIN EYE

Denise Fleming

SCHOLASTIC INC.

New York Toronto London Auckland Sydney
Mexico City New Delhi Hong Kong Buenos Aires

Yellow moon

rising soon...

piece of pie,
pumpkin
eye...

candlesticks,
burning
wicks.

Trick or treat—
pounding feet,
jack-o'-lanterns
line the street.

Down
the hill,

spirits

spill...

purple scales—
dragon tails,
twisted horns—
unicorns.

Trick
or treat—
pounding feet,
eerie
shadows
fill the street.

Swooping bats,
hissing cats...

tattered rags,
toothless hags,
pointed tails,
blood-red nails.

Trick or treat—
pounding feet,
wretched witches
roam the street.

Clacking bones,

muffled moans...

tigers
growl,

toes curl,
heads swirl,
things bump,
hearts thump.

Trick
or treat—

pounding feet,
Halloween
has found **our** street.